Fur will be flying!

Nancy looked around in wonder. There were cats and kittens everywhere: running around, sleeping on old rugs, eating and drinking out of big bowls. Bags of cat food and cat litter were heaped in one corner. Against one wall were a dozen steel cages, each with a cat curled up inside.

"Some of them are sick and need to be alone," Terry explained, pointing to the cages. "Some of them just don't get along with other cats. They're kind of like schoolyard bullies."

"Where do you find all these cats?" George asked her.

"Well, for starters, some of them have been abandoned by their owners," Terry began. Bess gasped. "What kind of people would abandon their kitty-cats?" she cried out.

The Nancy Drew Notebooks

# 1 The Slumber Party Secret	#36 The Make-Believe Mystery
# 2 The Lost Locket	#37 Dude Ranch Detective
# 3 The Secret Santa	#38 Candy Is Dandy
# 4 Bad Day for Ballet	#39 The Chinese New Year Mystery
# 5 The Soccer Shoe Clue	#40 Dinosaur Alert!
# 6 The Ice Cream Scoop	#41 Flower Power
# 7 Trouble at Camp Treehouse	#42 Circus Act
# 8 The Best Detective	#43 The Walkie-talkie Mystery
# 9 The Thanksgiving Surprise	#44 The Purple Fingerprint
#10 Not Nice on Ice	#45 The Dashing Dog Mystery
#11 The Pen Pal Puzzle	#46 The Snow Queen's Surprise
#12 The Puppy Problem	#47 The Crook Who Took the Book
#13 The Wedding Gift Goof	#48 The Crazy Carnival Case
#14 The Funny Face Fight	#49 The Sand Castle Mystery
#15 The Crazy Key Clue	#50 The Scarytales Sleepover
#16 The Ski Slope Mystery	#51 The Old-Fashioned Mystery
#17 Whose Pet Is Best?	#52 Big Worry in Wonderland
#18 The Stolen Unicorn	#53 Recipe for Trouble
#19 The Lemonade Raid	#54 The Stinky Cheese Surprise
#20 Hannah's Secret	#55 The Day Camp Disaster
#21 Princess on Parade	#56 Turkey Trouble
#22 The Clue in the Glue	#57 The Carousel Mystery
#23 Alien in the Classroom	#58 The Dollhouse Mystery
#24 The Hidden Treasures	#59 The Bike Race Mystery
#25 Dare at the Fair	#60 The Lighthouse Mystery
#26 The Lucky Horseshoes	#61 Space Case
#27 Trouble Takes the Cake	#62 The Secret in the Spooky Woods
#28 Thrill on the Hill	#63 Snowman Surprise
#29 Lights! Camera! Clues!	#64 Bunny-Hop Hoax
#30 It's No Joke!	#65 Strike-Out Scare
#31 The Fine-Feathered Mystery	#66 Zoo Clue
#32 The Black Velvet Mystery	#67 The Singing Suspects
#33 The Gumdrop Ghost	#68 The Apple Bandit
#34 Trash or Treasure?	#69 The Kitten Caper
#35 Third-Grade Reporter	

Available from Simon & Schuster

THE
NANCY DREW
NOTEBOOKS®

#69

The Kitten Caper

CAROLYN KEENE
ILLUSTRATED BY JAN NAIMO JONES

Aladdin Paperbacks
New York   London   Toronto   Sydney

This book is a work of fiction. Any references to historical events, real people, or real locales are used fictitiously. Other names, characters, places, and incidents are the product of the author's imagination, and any resemblance to actual events or locales or persons, living or dead, is entirely coincidental.

❧ ALADDIN PAPERBACKS
An imprint of Simon & Schuster Children's Publishing Division
1230 Avenue of the Americas, New York, NY 10020
Copyright © 2005 by Simon & Schuster, Inc
All rights reserved, including the right of reproduction in whole or in part in any form.
NANCY DREW and THE NANCY DREW NOTEBOOKS are registered trademarks of Simon & Schuster, Inc.
ALADDIN PAPERBACKS and colophon are trademarks of Simon & Schuster, Inc.
Designed by Lisa Vega
The text of this book was set in Excelsior.
Manufactured in the United States of America
First Aladdin Paperbacks Edition December 2005
10 9 8 7 6 5 4 3 2 1
Library of Congress Control Number 2005907547
ISBN-13: 978-1-4169-0830-2
ISBN-10: 1-4169-0830-7

The Kitten Caper

1

Furball Farm

Kitty-cats rule," eight-year-old Bess Marvin declared. "They're so fluffy and adorable."

"I agree," her cousin George Fayne said. "Nancy, what's your favorite kind of pet?"

Nancy Drew kicked some powdery snow with her boot as the three girls headed down the sidewalk. "Well, Chip is my favorite pet in the whole wide world," she said. Chocolate Chip was her brown Labrador retriever puppy. "After Chip, cats are definitely number two," she added.

"I wonder how many kitty-cats Terry Smith has?" Bess said. "Fifty? A hundred?"

"A million zillion?" George joked.

"She would need a *lot* of cat food to feed that many cats." Nancy giggled.

Nancy and her friends were on their way to visit Terry Smith, who lived around the corner from Nancy and her father. Terry rescued stray cats and kittens and took care of them until she could find them new homes.

The girls had been given a fun school assignment to do during winter break. They were supposed to interview someone with an interesting hobby. Nancy had heard about Terry from a neighbor. She, George, and Bess had decided that Terry would be the perfect person to interview. What could be a more interesting—or important— hobby than rescuing stray kitties?

Nancy had called Terry last week to set up an appointment to visit her. The woman had agreed right away. Nancy couldn't wait to meet her and all the kitties, too!

The girls soon reached Terry's house. It was lavender with purple shutters and had a big, sloping, snow-covered roof. There was a banner hanging above the front door with a picture of a black-and-white cat and the words MEOW! WELCOME!

Nancy proceeded to the front door through a heavy blanket of snow, followed by George and Bess. When Nancy rang the doorbell, she could hear a series of chimes inside: *Meow, meow, meow, meow!*

"I don't think Chip would like this place," Bess whispered.

A woman opened the door. She had long, wavy brown hair and friendly brown eyes. She wore a colorful patchwork dress, thick purple tights, and matching purple boots.

"Welcome!" the woman exclaimed. "You must be Nancy, George, and Bess. I'm Terry Smith. Well, my full name is Theresa Aspidistra Smith. But my friends just call me Terry. That's what you should call me too."

"Aspi-what?" George asked her. "It's a cool name, but it's hard to pronounce."

"As-pi-dis-tra," Terry repeated. "It's a kind of plant. My parents studied plants for a living. Me, I like to study things that move around and make noise. Like cats!"

Nancy reached into the pocket of her

3

parka and pulled out a small notebook and pen. She wanted to write this down as background information for their interview.

Terry held the door wide open. "You must be freezing cold. Come in! I'm sorry the walk isn't shoveled. With all my cats to take care of, I never seem to have time to do anything else."

Nancy and her friends stomped the snow off their boots and entered the house. In the front hall, they were greeted by a large cat with long, golden fur. The kitty brushed up against Nancy's leg and meowed loudly.

"That's Mr. Wigglesworth," Terry said. "Those two over there on top of the radiator are Ruffles and Rufus. That's General Dave racing down the hall. And there are Fanny, Ming-a-Ling, Maud, and Gray Mouse right behind him."

There were cats everywhere! Terry continued pointing them out and introducing them to the girls: Baxter, Fairycake Jones, Bonnie Blue, Mrs. Dinnertime, and Blossom. There was even a one-eyed cat called Cyclops, named after the one-eyed beast from the Greek myth.

"Wow, you have a lot of cats," Nancy said to Terry.

"Oh, this is just a few of them," Terry said with a shrug. "Most of my rescue cats are in the barn."

"They are?" Bess said, her blue eyes wide.

Terry nodded. "Yes. Let me show you the barn. No, General Dave, you can't go out! Bad kitty!" she said, shaking her finger at a fuzzy gray cat. "This way, girls."

Terry pulled on a long, black sweater and headed out the front door. Nancy and her friends followed. Nancy saw that Terry's sweater had lots of scraggly-looking loose threads coming out of it. It was also covered with cat fur.

Terry noticed Nancy's glance. "The cats love this sweater," she said with a grin. "Whenever I wear it, they sit on me, roll around on me, and use me as a scratching post."

"A scratching post! Doesn't that hurt?" Bess asked her curiously.

Terry shook her head. "Nah. I'm used to it. I'm even used to having all my clothes look furry and bedraggled."

Terry led the girls through the snow-covered yard. Icicles glistened in the December sun. A cardinal perched on a pine branch and fluttered its wings. Otherwise, everything was peaceful and still.

They eventually came to a large barn out back. It was painted the same color purple as the main house.

"Here we are!" Terry announced.

She opened the barn door. Inside it was neither peaceful nor still. Dozens of cats and kittens rushed up to the door, meowing like crazy.

"Quick, get inside, before the devilish little fiends escape," Terry said, smiling at Nancy and her friends. The girls obeyed hastily.

Terry closed the door and turned to them, grinning. "Welcome to Furball Farm!"

Nancy looked around in wonder. There were cats and kittens everywhere: running around, sleeping on old rugs, eating and drinking out of big bowls. Bags of cat food and cat litter were heaped in one corner. Against one wall were a dozen steel cages, each with a cat curled up inside.

"Some of them are sick and need to be alone," Terry explained, pointing to the cages. "Some of them just don't get along with other cats. They're kind of like school-yard bullies."

"Where do you find all these cats?" George asked her.

"Well, for starters, some of them have been abandoned by their owners," Terry began.

Bess gasped. "What kind of people would abandon their kitty-cats?" she cried out.

Nancy pulled her notebook and pen out of her pocket. She wanted to write all this down.

Terry smiled sadly. "You'd be surprised. People who move away and don't want to take their cats with them. People who adopt a cat, only to find out that they're not ready for pet ownership. People who realize that their new cat doesn't get along with their old cat or dog. The list goes on and on."

Nancy glanced up from her notebook. "But why would they abandon their cats? Why wouldn't they try to find a new home for them?" she asked Terry.

"That's a very good question," Terry

replied. "Some people aren't very smart or responsible when it comes to pet ownership."

Nancy thought about Chip. She would never abandon Chip in a million years—no matter what!

"Anyway, some of these cats were abandoned and became strays," Terry went on. "Some of them were born from other strays, so they've always lived outside. They never knew what it was like to live in a cozy home." She added, "They come to my door. Or people find them roaming in their neighborhoods and bring them to me. People who know me know that I can't say no to a stray cat."

"So you just keep all of them?" George asked her.

"I try to find new homes for as many as I can," Terry replied. "If I can't find homes for them, they're welcome to live here at Furball Farm. The barn has heat, electricity, the works. Or the cats can live in my house, if I have room."

Just then, a pair of kittens rushed up to Bess and began sniffing her red boots. One of them was chocolate brown with a dark brown tail and ears. The other one was cream-colored with a pinkish tail and ears. They had identical deep blue eyes.

"Oh, they're so cute!" Bess exclaimed.

"The dark one is Cocoa, and the light one is Creampuff," Terry said. "I found them last week, hungry and shivering in the woods out back. I think they're brother and sister."

"Awwww." Bess sat down on the floor. Cocoa and Creampuff immediately jumped onto her lap and began licking her hand.

"They're totally adorable," Nancy agreed. She reached down to pet the brown one, Cocoa. Cocoa gave a tiny meow and rubbed against Nancy's fingertips. Nancy could feel the little kitten purring happily, like a motor.

"How old are they?" Nancy asked Terry.

"I think they're about three months old, or maybe—" Terry was interrupted by a knock on the barn door.

"Probably someone with another stray cat," Terry said. "Come in!" she called out loudly.

The door opened, and a man walked in. He was tall and big-shouldered, with round

pink cheeks. Curly blond hair peeked out from underneath his massive fur hat.

"Good afternoon, Ms. Smith," the man said, smiling at Terry. He ignored Nancy and her friends.

"Hello, Mr. Layton," Terry replied. She sounded confused. "What are you doing here? I thought—"

"I came by to see if you've had a chance to reconsider my offer," Mr. Layton cut in smoothly.

Terry shook her head. "It's like I told you yesterday. Creampuff and Cocoa aren't for sale."

Creampuff and Cocoa? What was this about? Nancy glanced worriedly at the two little kittens.

"I'll double my price," Mr. Layton insisted.

Terry shook her head again. "My answer is still the same, Mr. Layton. Creampuff and Cocoa are not for sale."

Mr. Layton's smile froze on his face. His mouth twisted into a snarl. "Then you're going to be very, very sorry," he said in a nasty voice.

2

Mr. Layton Returns

Mr. Layton stared at Cocoa and Cream-puff, who were curled up on Bess's lap. Then he stormed out the door. A cold wind gusted in as he left. Nancy shivered.

A scruffy-looking orange cat meowed loudly at Terry. "Yes, Pumpkin, I know. It's dinnertime," she said. She sounded distracted, as though she were deep in thought.

"What does that man want with Cocoa and Creampuff?" Nancy asked Terry.

"And why was he so mean to you?" George added.

Terry lifted a big bag of cat food from the floor and began pouring it into large metal bowls. Cats and kittens swarmed around her ankles, meowing like crazy.

"That man is Michael Layton. He breeds, buys, and sells fancy cats as a business," Terry explained.

Nancy nodded. It made sense now. "And he wants to buy Cocoa and Creampuff from you," she said.

"Exactly," Terry replied. "He came by yesterday and offered me a lot of money for them. But I told him then what I told him just now: Cocoa and Creampuff aren't for sale." She added, "I don't know why he's interested in them. They're stray cats, not some sort of special breed."

Bess looked up, frowning. "But I thought you *wanted* to find new homes for all your rescue cats."

"I do," Terry said. "But Cocoa and Creampuff deserve to find a cozy home together with loving parents. There's a good chance Mr. Layton would sell them to separate owners. Or, even if he sold them to one owner, that new owner could then turn around and sell them to separate owners. The people in Mr. Layton's world are businesspeople, not cat people. Cocoa and Creampuff need to stay together!"

Nancy glanced at the two kittens, who were eating some cat food side by side with their tails intertwined. She couldn't imagine the brother and sister being apart.

Nancy turned her attention back to her notebook and wrote all this down. The three girls continued asking Terry questions about Furball Farm for the next half hour. Then it was time to go home.

"Please come back tomorrow afternoon if you can," Terry said as she bid them good-bye. "From two to four, I'm having a holiday open house here at Furball Farm. It's a chance for people who might be interested in adopting a kitty to come meet all my little guys. Also, I get a chance to ask people for donations, like cat food and litter and stuff like that."

The three girls looked at one another, smiling. "We'll have to ask our parents first. But we'd love to come!" Bess said. Nancy and George nodded eagerly.

The next day Nancy, Bess, and George arrived at Furball Farm exactly at two thirty. Their parents had given them permission to attend Terry Smith's holiday open house.

"It looks like a lot of people are here," Nancy noted. She pointed to all the cars parked on the street in front of Terry's house and in her driveway.

"It would be so cool if they all wanted to adopt one of Terry's kitties!" George said. She jumped into a pile of snow and jumped back out again.

"Especially Cocoa and Creampuff," Bess said. "I really hope they find a good home. I asked my mom and dad if I could adopt them, but they said no. They said maybe one cat, but not two. And Cocoa and Creampuff have to stay together."

The girls reached the barn and went inside. It looked totally different than it had yesterday. There were holiday decorations all over the walls: wreaths with red and green kitty toys on them, and garlands made

15

of holly and mistletoe. There was a CD of "Jingle Bells"—sung by cats!—blasting from a portable CD player.

About twenty or thirty people were milling around the barn. They were talking, petting the kitties, and nibbling on cat-shaped cookies. Nancy recognized a few of them from the neighborhood.

"Hello, girls!"

Terry came hurrying over to Nancy, George, and Bess. She was wearing a long denim dress with sequined cat designs all over it.

"I'm so glad you could make it!" she exclaimed happily. "Here, have a cookie!" she added, extending a tray piled high with delicious-looking treats.

Bess took a cookie. "We wouldn't have missed it for anything!" she replied. "Mmm, this cookie is yummy."

"Plus, it's research," George said. She pulled a notebook and pen out of her pocket. The three girls had agreed to take turns jotting down notes for their school project. "We thought we might interview some of your guests," George told Terry.

"What a great idea," Terry said.

Just then, a girl rushed up to Terry. She had long, golden brown hair and was dressed in jeans and a pink top. She looked like a teenager to Nancy.

"Hey, Terry?" the girl said breathlessly. "That lady over there with the big nose and the weird blue hat says she might want to adopt a couple of cats."

"Ella!" Terry whispered. "Don't insult the guests, okay?"

The girl hung her head. "Uh, okay. Sorry."

Terry sighed. "Girls, this is my assistant, Ella Gurney," she said. "She works part-time for me after school. Ella, this is Nancy, George, and Bess. They're doing a story about me."

"Oh, wow. Cool," Ella said.

"Why don't you introduce me to the woman with the big—I mean, the woman who wants to adopt a couple of cats?" Terry suggested to Ella. "Excuse me, girls."

"Sure," Nancy said.

Terry and Ella walked away. "I wonder where Cocoa and Creampuff are?" Bess said, glancing around.

"You mean Turboslayer and Titan?" a boy's voice spoke up.

The three girls turned around. A boy was standing there. He had short, dark brown hair and brown eyes. He was holding Cocoa and Creampuff in his arms. The kittens wore matching red collars with silver bells.

"Hi, kitties!" Bess squeaked. She reached over to pet them. "Wait. Turboslayer and Titan?" she asked the boy.

The boy nodded eagerly. "Turboslayer and Titan are my favorite characters from my favorite comic book and TV show, *Destroyers of Doom*. That's what I'm going to name these guys—if my mom lets me adopt them."

Then he frowned. "My mom said no the first twenty-four times I asked, though. But maybe twenty-five will be my lucky number." He grinned, revealing a mouthful of blue-tinted braces.

Nancy and her friends exchanged a glance. "I'm Nancy, and these are my friends George and Bess," she said to him.

The boy introduced himself as Richie Feathers. He told the girls that he was in sixth grade at a nearby private school. He also said that he lived right next door to Terry, on the other side of a clump of trees.

"Why won't your mom let you have a cat, Richie?" Bess asked. Nancy could tell Bess felt bad for him.

"She's super allergic to cats," Richie explained. "They make her sneeze and get really watery eyes and stuff like that."

Richie paused and smiled confidently. "I've been doing lots of research on the Internet, though," he went on. "I'm trying to find her a cure for cat allergies. Did you know that back in the old days, people used to chew on a piece of honeycomb to cure allergies? Like gum? Maybe that would work for my mom."

"Uh, yeah," George said doubtfully.

"Excuse me," a man's voice interrupted.

It was Mr. Layton. He tapped Richie on the shoulder. "I need to borrow those felines from you for a second," he said.

"Felines?" Richie repeated. "You mean cats?"

A woman was standing next to Mr. Layton. "My, they're precious, aren't they, Michael?" she exclaimed.

The woman was dressed in a strange-looking fur coat. Bess stared at it, her blue eyes wide. "Is—is that made of cats?" she blurted out.

The woman gasped. "Of course not! It's fake fur."

"Oh! I'm sorry," Bess apologized.

"The felines. Now." Mr. Layton reached over and plucked Cocoa and Creampuff out of Richie's arms. The kittens squealed in protest.

"Hey!" Richie cried out.

Mr. Layton handed Cocoa to the woman. Then he lifted Creampuff in the air and stretched her body long, as though she were a piece of dough. "See the bone structure? The markings?" he said.

"Remarkable," the woman agreed.

Creampuff squealed again. She wriggled restlessly.

"Stop that! You're hurting her!" Bess cried out.

"I'm not hurting her in the least," Mr. Layton replied.

Just then, Terry came walking over. "Mr. Layton. Mrs. Layton. What can I do for you?" she said in a tense-sounding voice.

"Let's discuss this in private," Mr. Layton said. "This is an adult conversation." He glanced at Nancy, Bess, George, and Richie.

Terry and the Laytons walked away, with the couple carrying Cocoa and Creampuff. Nancy frowned. Was Mr. Layton still trying to buy the two kittens from Terry?

"That guy better not try to adopt Titan and Turboslayer," Richie said, glaring at Mr. Layton. "They're *my* cats. No one is going to get them but me!"

"*If* your mom says yes," Nancy reminded him.

Richie's shoulders slumped. "Yeah. If."

Nancy, George, and Bess were the last ones to leave the party. They stuck around to help Terry clean up, since Terry's assistant Ella wasn't around. Ella had left earlier to visit her great-aunt in a nursing home.

"What a wonderful party this was!" Terry exclaimed as she picked up a pile of fliers.

"Did you find new homes for any of your cats?" Nancy asked her.

"Fifteen new homes!" Terry replied. "All with very nice people. I also raised lots of money to buy cat food and litter. Oh, and I met a local veterinarian who is going to do some volunteer work for Furball Farm."

"How about Creampuff and Cocoa?" Bess said slowly. "Did . . . did Mr. Layton and his wife buy them from you?"

Terry shook her head. "I told him no. Again. He doesn't seem like the kind of person who gives up easily, though," she said with a sigh.

Nancy glanced around. "Speaking of Creampuff and Cocoa . . . where are they?" she asked Terry.

Terry looked around too. "Creampuff! Cocoa! Come here, kitties!" she sang out.

Half a dozen cats raced up to Terry. But Creampuff and Cocoa weren't among them.

"Creampuff! Cocoa!" Terry repeated, more loudly. "That's strange. They always come when I call," she told the girls.

Nancy frowned.

Were Creampuff and Cocoa missing?

3

Kit-napped!

Creampuff! Cocoa! Kitties! Come here right now!"

Terry wandered through the barn, calling out to the kittens. Nancy, Bess, and George did the same.

"Where could they be?" Bess asked worriedly as she peered under a chair.

"Maybe they're hiding somewhere," George suggested. She peeked behind a cupboard.

"I don't know. They don't often hide. They like to run around and play with the other cats," Terry said. "Creampuff! Cocoa!" she yelled.

Nancy searched under the cages. She looked behind the bags of cat food and litter. She checked in all the nooks and crevices of the barn.

She found lots of kitties in these hiding places. But Cocoa and Creampuff were not among them.

Nancy turned to Terry. "Do you think they got outside by accident?" she asked her.

"It's possible," Terry replied. "So many people have been coming and going these last couple of hours."

"Let's check it out," Nancy suggested. "Bess, you stay in the barn and keep looking."

Bess nodded. "Okay."

Nancy, George, and Terry put on their coats and went outside. They closed the barn door carefully so none of the cats or kittens would follow them.

Terry headed into the snow. But Nancy put her hand out to stop her.

"Pawprints," Nancy said. "If the kitties got away, there would be pawprints in the snow. It snowed this morning and stopped around lunchtime, so the snow out here is fresh. We should look for any pawprints that might be here before we erase them with our own footprints."

"Wow, you talk just like a real detective," Terry said, sounding impressed.

"Nancy *is* a real detective," George said proudly. "She's the best detective at Carl Sandburg Elementary School. She's solved lots of mysteries!"

"Well, I certainly hope she can solve the mystery of my two missing kittens," Terry said.

Nancy bent down and began studying the marks in the snow. There were dozens and dozens of footprints, no doubt from the party guests. They all went to and from the driveway and the street.

One set of footprints cut through Terry's yard toward the neighbor's yard. Nancy noted that the prints weren't that much bigger than her own. *They must belong to Richie Feathers*, she guessed. *He said he lived right next door to Terry.*

Nancy continued to study the marks in the snow. Even though there were lots of footprints, there were no pawprints at all—not near the barn, not near the house, not anywhere in the yard.

"It doesn't look like Creampuff and Cocoa ran out of the barn," Nancy said finally. "At least, I don't see any pawprints anywhere."

"Why don't we go back inside? Maybe Bess had better luck than we did," Terry said hopefully.

The three of them went back into the barn. There, they found Bess on the floor. She was poking around under an old wooden table.

"Bess?" Nancy said curiously. "Did you find the kittens?"

Bess shimmied out from under the table. She was covered with cat fur and dust. "No, but I found these," she said.

Bess held up two red collars with silver bells attached to them. "Creampuff and Cocoa were wearing collars just like these at the party," she pointed out.

"Did any other cats have collars like those?" Nancy asked Terry quickly.

Terry shook her head. "No. Just Creampuff

and Cocoa," she replied. "I made those collars especially for them, for the party."

"How did they get off the kitties and under this table?" George piped up.

Nancy glanced at George, then Bess, then Terry. "Someone must have *taken* them off the kittens," she said in a serious voice. "The same someone who may have kidnapped them."

On Sunday morning after breakfast, Nancy, George, and Bess returned to Furball Farm. They wanted to see if the missing kitties might have turned up during the night.

But when they got there, Terry had no such good news for them. In fact, she looked tired, with dark circles under her eyes.

"I've been up since five a.m. looking for them," Terry told the girls. "I even left out a bowl of their favorite treat, strawberries. But they didn't come."

"Strawberries?" Bess exclaimed. "They like strawberries?"

Terry nodded. "Some cats like fruit. Some cats like vegetables. You'd be surprised. I once knew a cat who liked cantaloupe and raw green beans."

Nancy noticed that Ella was in the corner, cleaning out some cages. "Hi, Ella," she called out.

Ella turned around and waved. She had a roll of paper towels in one hand and a bottle of cleaning spray in the other. "Hey," she said.

"You haven't seen Creampuff and Cocoa, have you?" Nancy asked her.

Ella shook her head. "Nope. I can't believe they're missing! I told Terry I'd help her try to find them. I'm good at finding things. I'm always losing my CDs and earrings and schoolbooks and stuff, but then I find them again. Well, most of the time."

Terry turned to Nancy and her friends. Her brown eyes were shiny with tears. "Oh, girls, who could have taken those poor little kitties?" she said with a moan.

Just then, something caught Nancy's eye. It was a shiny, crumpled-up piece of paper on the floor next to the garbage can. She could make out the symbols "$$$" on it, written in green ink.

She walked over to the piece of paper and picked it up. A scruffy black cat came up to her and rubbed against her ankles, purring. "Hi, kitty," she said. "I don't have time to pet you right now."

Nancy smoothed the paper out carefully and scraped some dried mud off of it. She studied it closely. It seemed to be a page torn from a magazine.

In the center of the page was a photograph of a cat. Nancy gasped. The cat looked a lot like Creampuff and Cocoa!

Some words were written in green Magic Marker along the side of the paper: "Same breed? Ragdoll, Seal, Lilac. If so, worth $$$. Call Roger—I can get 2 right away."

"What is it, Nancy?" Bess asked her.

Nancy walked over to the others and showed them the piece of paper. "Is this yours?" she asked Terry.

Terry shook her head. "No. And that's not my handwriting, either." She added, "The cat in this picture looks a lot like Creampuff and Cocoa!"

"Definitely," Bess agreed.

Nancy's thoughts were racing. Did some-one steal Creampuff and Cocoa, because they might be the same breed as the cat in the magazine? Did that same someone want to sell the two kitties to a person named Roger for lots of money?

Could that someone be Michael Layton?

4

Behind the Blue Door

Nancy stared hard at the new clue. Michael Layton really wanted Creampuff and Cocoa. He came to Furball Farm to try to convince Terry to sell them to him—not once, not twice, but three times. He even told Terry that she would be very, very sorry if she didn't.

"Could Mr. Layton be our kitty thief?" Nancy said out loud to Terry.

"Mr. Layton?" Terry repeated. She sounded shocked. "Why on Earth would he steal my kittens?"

George's eyes lit up. "You're right, Nancy. Mr. Layton must be the thief!"

"He really wanted to buy Cocoa and Creampuff from you," Bess reminded Terry. "And you kept saying no. Maybe he decided the only solution was kit-napping!"

"I don't know," Terry said uncertainly. "He's a well-known and respected cat breeder. He's not the most polite or pleasant person in the world. But I can't believe he's a criminal!"

Nancy noticed that Ella had stopped cleaning the cages and was listening to their conversation. "Ella, do you know anything about this?" she asked, holding up the piece of paper.

Ella shook her head. "I've never seen it before. I bet you're right, though. I bet that Layton guy is the thief!" she said firmly.

Ella sounded pretty sure. So did Bess and George. Nancy still needed more proof, though.

Nancy pointed to the handwritten words on the page. "Ragdoll. Seal. Lilac. What do they mean?" she asked Geroge and Bess.

"Hmm. I'm not sure," George said after a moment. "I mean, we all know that a rag doll is a kind of doll. And a seal is a kind of

34

sea animal. And a lilac is a kind of flower. Other than that . . ." She paused and shrugged.

Nancy stared and stared at the words.

A doll. A sea animal. A flower.

Was this puzzle the key to the mystery of Creampuff and Cocoa? If so, what did it mean?

"Okay, what words did you want to search again?" Hannah Gruen asked Nancy.

Nancy scooted closer to Hannah in front of the family computer. Hannah was the Drews' housekeeper. But she was way more than a housekeeper. She had helped take care of Nancy since Nancy's mother died five years ago.

Nancy took a sip of the yummy hot chocolate that Hannah had prepared for her. She made sure to keep the mug far away from the computer.

"Ragdoll, seal, and lilac," Nancy told Hannah.

"Hmm, sounds like you're right in the middle of another mystery," Hannah said, her eyes twinkling.

"I am!" Nancy replied. She told Hannah all about the missing kittens.

"The poor things," Hannah said when Nancy had finished. "But with you on the case, I'm sure they'll turn up very soon," she added, squeezing Nancy's arm.

"I hope so," Nancy said.

Hannah typed some words to call up a search engine. A search engine was a computer program that could find facts and track down information.

The search-engine page popped up on the screen. There was a cartoon detective with a magnifying glass. Above her head, it read: HI, I'M DETECTIVE DAPHNE DESKTOP. WHAT CAN I FIND FOR YOU TODAY?

"She looks like you, Nancy," Hannah joked.

Nancy giggled.

Hannah typed in "ragdoll," "seal," and "lilac." A few seconds later, a new page popped up on the screen. Hannah typed a few more words. Yet another new page popped up.

Across the top of the page were the words WELCOME TO THE WORLD OF FANCY CATS.

Underneath the welcome message was a photograph of a cat. Nancy gasped. The cat looked like Creampuff and Cocoa—and like the cat on the piece of paper Nancy had found at Furball Farm! This particular cat was chocolate brown with dark brown ears, like Cocoa.

"This is it!" Nancy cried out. "Can you go down the page, Hannah?"

Hannah punched a key and scrolled down the page. There was a description of the cat under the photograph:

Bon Bon is a classic ragdoll cat, owned by Miguel and Patty Gonzalez of Austin, Texas. Ragdolls make ideal pets because of their sweet, social, almost teddy bear–like personalities. Notice that Bon Bon has beautiful seal points.

"There's the word 'seal,'" Nancy said excitedly. She jabbed her finger at the screen. "It must have something to do with the way the cat looks. What are 'points,' anyway?"

"Let's find out," Hannah said.

She and Nancy continued reading more articles on the Web site. Within fifteen minutes, Nancy had learned everything she needed to know. "Points" were colorful markings on a cat. A cat could have dark points on its tail, ears, face, and elsewhere. "Seal" and "lilac" described some of the colors. Seal points were dark brown. Lilac points were pinkish.

Nancy thought about this new information. Cocoa had dark brown ears and a dark brown tail: seal points. Creampuff had pinkish ears and a pinkish tail: lilac points.

The handwritten words on the magazine page she had found at Furball Farm definitely had something to do with the missing kittens, she concluded.

Someone thought that Cocoa and Creampuff were a special breed of cats called ragdolls. Terry had told Nancy that Michael Layton sold fancy cat breeds.

It was time to pay Michael Layton a visit.

"Is this the right address?" Hannah asked Nancy.

Nancy glanced at the computer printout with Michael Layton's address. "Layton's Fine Felines. Twenty-eight Rockwell Street. This is it."

Hannah parked her car in front of a large, elegant-looking brick mansion. Nancy, George, and Bess got out from the backseat.

"I'll wait here for you girls while you interrogate the witness," Hannah said with a wink. "Or whatever it is you detectives do."

"Thanks, Hannah," Nancy said, smiling.

She walked along a snow-covered path to the front of the mansion, her friends following. There was a small gold-plated sign on the front door. It read: FOR LAYTON'S FINE FELINES, PLEASE GO AROUND TO THE BACK.

The girls went around the mansion to the back. When they got there, they found a young man shoveling snow. "Can I help you girls?" he called out.

"We're here to see Mr. Layton," Nancy replied.

"He's in the main house. He should be right back. Feel free to go inside the cattery and wait for him," the man said.

"Thank you!" the girls said in unison.

"What's a cattery?" Bess whispered to Nancy.

"I think it's another name for, you know, a cat store or whatever," Nancy whispered back.

The three of them opened an antique-looking wooden door marked LAYTON'S FINE FELINES and went inside to an enormous office. In the middle of the office was a large marble desk and chair. All along the walls were dozens of silver cages. Inside each cage was a cat.

Nancy had never seen such unusual-looking cats before. There was a gray-and-white cat with a pointy nose and huge, batlike ears. The sign on its cage read BREED, CORNISH REX. There was a tall, slender, silver cat with black spots, like a leopard. The sign on its cage said BREED, EGYPTIAN MAU.

The girls saw other exotic breeds with interesting names like Australian Mist, American Curl, and Brazilian Shorthair. There was even a completely hairless cat called a sphynx!

40

Bess stared over Nancy's shoulder at the sphynx. "I've never seen a bald cat before," she said.

Just then, Nancy noticed something. In the back corner of the office was a blue door marked PRIVATE.

She walked up to the door and pressed her ear against it. She could hear tiny meows coming from the other side. They sounded like kittens.

"What is it, Nancy?" George asked her. She and Bess had followed her to the blue door.

"Listen," Nancy whispered.

They heard more meows.

Could the meowing kittens be Creampuff and Cocoa? Nancy wondered.

She put her hand on the doorknob and began to turn it.

"What do you think you're doing?" a voice said behind her.

5

A Suspicious Sneeze

Nancy and her friends whirled around. Mrs. Layton was standing there. She was dressed in a different fur coat than the one she had been wearing at Terry Smith's open house.

"We're, um, here to see Mr. Layton," Nancy said innocently. "The man outside told us to wait for him. We thought Mr. Layton might be in here."

"Well, he most certainly is not," Mrs. Layton said huffily. "Can't you read? That door says 'Private.' Private means little girls can't go barging in there."

"We're sorry, we didn't know," George piped up.

Mrs. Layton frowned. "Why do you want to see my husband, anyway?"

"Um, well." Nancy thought. "We wanted to ask him about some cats."

"My mom is thinking of buying one of those stinks cats," Bess fibbed.

Mrs. Layton raised one eyebrow. "You mean the sphynx?"

"That's right." Bess nodded.

The blue door opened suddenly, making Nancy and her friends jump. Mr. Layton walked through, holding two small, fuzzy kittens in his arms. They were gray and white—nothing like Creampuff and Cocoa.

Mr. Layton stopped and stared suspiciously at Nancy and her friends. "What are you three doing here, may I ask?" he said.

"Michael, they claim they're interested in a sphynx," Mrs. Layton said.

"Well, I don't do business with children. Go along, now. Good-bye!" Mr. Layton said with a wave of his hand. The kittens in his arms began meowing. Their meows

sounded like the ones Nancy had heard through the blue door.

Bess marched up to Mr. Layton and put her hands on her hips. "Did you steal Creampuff and Cocoa?" she blurted out.

"Bess!" Nancy cried out.

"Creampuff and who?" Mr. Layton said, looking puzzled. "What on Earth are you talking about?"

"The two kittens at Furball Farm," Nancy explained quickly. "The ragdolls."

"Ah, yes, them." Mr. Layton nodded. "Shame she wouldn't sell them to me. I offered her a lot of money. I was going to sell them to my friend Roger Doolittle for an excellent profit. He loves ragdoll cats, and those two specimens at Furball Farm seemed quite fine." Then he paused. "Did you say 'steal'? Why, are they missing?"

"Do you know where they are?" Nancy asked him.

Mr. Layton frowned. "Of course not. Why would I? I haven't seen—what did you call them, Coconut and Puffball?—since the open house yesterday."

"Cocoa and Creampuff." Bess corrected him.

"Yes, whatever. Anyway, I haven't seen them since yesterday. End of story. Now, if you children will be going along, I have important business to take care of."

Mr. Layton pointed to the door.

"Do you think Mr. Layton was telling the truth?" Bess asked Nancy as Hannah drove down Rockwell Street. Bess was sitting between Nancy and George in the backseat.

"He sounded like he was, but I'm not one hundred percent sure," Nancy replied.

"The Laytons are kind of nasty," George remarked.

"Yeah. But that doesn't mean they're thieves," Nancy pointed out.

"True," George said.

Bess sat up suddenly. "Turboslayer and Titan," she burst out.

Nancy and George turned to her. "Huh?" they said.

"That boy, Richie Feathers," Bess reminded her friends. "Remember? He really wanted to adopt Creampuff and Cocoa. He even had new names picked out for them. Turboslayer and Titan. What if *he* stole the kitties?"

Nancy thought for a moment. "But he said his mom was allergic to cats," she said.

"Maybe he decided to take them anyway," Bess said. "You know, before Mr. Layton or anyone else had a chance to."

Nancy nodded. "That's true. Why don't we go talk to him, then?"

"Agreed," George said.

Nancy asked Hannah to drop her, Bess, and George off at Richie Feathers's house. They promised to walk home afterward.

"Good luck!" Hannah said when she reached the Feathers's house. The girls thanked her and got out of the car. Hannah waved and drove off.

Nancy and her friends walked up to the front door. Nancy rang the doorbell.

After a moment, a pretty blond woman answered the door. "Hi, there," she said. "What can I do for—excuse me—*ahchoo*!" She turned her head and sneezed violently.

"Are you okay?" Nancy asked her.

The woman nodded. Then she sneezed again.

"We're looking for Richie," Bess piped up.

"That would be my son. He's—" Mrs. Feathers hesitated, then sneezed again. She reached into her jeans pocket and pulled out a crumpled-up tissue. "I am so sorry," she apologized. "I think it's my cat allergies."

Nancy frowned. She'd had the impression that the Feathers family didn't *have* any cats.

"How many cats do you have?" Nancy asked Mrs. Feathers curiously.

Mrs. Feathers smiled and shook her head. "We don't have any. That's the funny thing. There must be cat fur blowing over from Terry Smith's house next door. She has a lot of cats over there." She laughed, then sneezed again.

Nancy and her friends exchanged a glance. *Maybe it was cat fur blowing over from Terry's,* Nancy thought.

Or maybe Richie had sneaked a couple of cats into his house without his mother's knowledge. A couple of cats named Creampuff and Cocoa!

6

A Third Suspect?

At that moment Richie came trotting down the stairs. "Hi, Mom. Can I watch *Destroyers of Doom* now? Oh, hey," he said, suddenly noticing Nancy and her friends.

Mrs. Feathers sneezed again. "Yes. But first, these girls are here to see you. Girls, come on in."

Nancy and her friends stomped the snow off their boots and went inside. "We met you yesterday at Terry Smith's," Nancy reminded Richie with a smile.

"Right. Natalie, Georgia, and Beth, right?" Richie said.

"Nancy, George, and Bess," George corrected him.

Richie blushed. "Sorry. Hey, you want to watch *Destroyers of Doom* with me? It's on in two minutes. It's the episode when Turboslayer and Titan defend Jupiter City against the evil mind-controlled lizard clones."

"No, thanks," Nancy said. "Actually that's what we're here to talk to you about. Turboslayer and Titan."

"The kitties Turboslayer and Titan. Also known as Creampuff and Cocoa," Bess added.

"The ones at Terry Smith's," George said.

Richie got a panicked expression on his face. "I don't know what you're talking about," he said through clenched teeth.

He's hiding something, Nancy thought.

The cell phone in Mrs. Feathers's pocket began ringing. "Excuse me," she said. "I need to get that."

She disappeared down the hall. George turned to Richie. "You *are* the thief, then," she said triumphantly. "You stole Creampuff and Cocoa!"

"You snuck them into your house as secret

pets," Bess accused him. "Where are you hiding them? In your room? In the basement?"

Richie looked totally confused. "Secret pets? What are you talking about? You think I stole those kittens? I wouldn't do that."

"Then why did you get so upset when I brought them up?" Nancy asked him.

Richie glanced down the hall. "Good. She can't hear us. You almost blew my secret!" he said in a loud whisper.

"What secret?" Bess asked him.

Richie glanced down the hall again. "I have a super-secret plan to adopt some cats," he explained with a grin.

"What super-secret plan?" George demanded.

"I was doing some research online. And I found out about a breed of totally hairless cats," Richie replied.

"Oh, yeah. The stinks," Bess said, nodding.

Richie frowned. "The *sphynx*. They're called the sphynx. Anyway, I'm going to do some more research on them. Then I'm going to try to convince Mom and Dad to let me adopt a couple of them. They can't say no, right? If the cats are hairless, Mom can't be allergic to them, right?"

Nancy was silent as she considered this. Richie's story seemed like it could be true.

But there was one missing piece. "Why is your mom sneezing so much, then?" she asked Richie.

"I've been going over to Terry's a lot this week to play with her cats. My clothes get really covered with cat fur. I guess that's been making Mom kind of sneeze a lot." Richie blushed. "I guess I'd better start doing my own laundry."

Then he frowned. "Did you say Turbo-slayer and Titan are missing? I hope you find them soon."

"So do we," Nancy said.

"Pass the popcorn!"

"Pass the apple cider!"

"Pass the chocolate-chip cookies!"

Nancy, Bess, and George were sitting cross-legged on Nancy's bed. They were all dressed in warm, fuzzy pajamas.

They were having a sleepover at Nancy's house. Hannah had prepared lots of goodies for them to snack on. The girls passed the plates and trays around, munching happily.

53

Nancy's dog Chip was sleeping on the floor. Her tail thumped energetically against the carpet. *She must be dreaming about chasing cats,* Nancy thought, grinning.

"Let's go over our suspects so far," George suggested.

"Michael Layton and Richie Feathers," Bess said. She took a handful of popcorn and popped it into her mouth.

"And they both say they're innocent," Nancy said thoughtfully.

Nancy reached over to her desk and pulled a blue notebook out of the top drawer. Her father had given her the notebook to keep track of her mysteries.

She opened it to a blank page. Picking up a pen, she wrote:

THE MYSTERY OF THE MISSING KITTENS

Missing: Creampuff and Cocoa

Suspect #1: Michael Layton. He offered to buy the kittens from Terry Smith for a lot of money, but she said no.

Suspect #2: Richie Feathers. He really

wanted to adopt the kittens, even though his mom said no.

Clues: The two red collars that belonged to the kittens, with silver bells on them. A page torn out of a magazine with words on it.

Nancy stared and stared at what she had just written. Sometimes, just seeing the facts of a case on paper gave her fresh new ideas.

"The red collars," Nancy said suddenly. "Why did the thief take them off the kitties?"

"Because he didn't like the color red?" Bess joked.

"Because the bells made noise," George said, jumping to her feet. "The thief wanted to sneak the kittens out of the barn without anyone hearing them."

Nancy held her pen up in the air. "Exactly!"

"So we're talking about a pretty smart thief," George mused.

Nancy nodded. "I think we should pay another visit to Furball Farm tomorrow. Maybe we can find more clues that will help us find our smart thief."

• • •

The next morning was cloudy and gray. It looked like it might start snowing at any minute.

Nancy, Bess, and George trekked through Terry Smith's backyard. Terry was in the house, busily feeding General Dave and the other house cats. She told Nancy and her friends to go back to the barn, and she would meet them there in a few minutes.

Bess stared out at the snowy woods behind the barn. "Poor Creampuff and Cocoa. What if they're out there somewhere, shivering in the cold?"

"I don't think they're out there. I think they're inside in some cozy place—with our cat thief," Nancy replied.

They got to the barn. Nancy opened the door. Lots of cats and kittens began meowing.

But above the din of the kitties, Nancy heard someone talking. The person sounded angry.

"You can't tell anyone where those two kittens came from!" the person cried out.

7

Caught in the Act

Nancy stopped and put her finger to her lips. "Shhh," she whispered to Bess and George.

Nancy closed the barn door behind her quietly. She glanced around—and saw Ella in the corner. Terry's assistant had a cell phone pressed to her ear.

Nancy's thoughts were racing. *You can't tell anyone where those two kittens came from,* Ella had said to the person on the other end of the phone. Was Ella talking about Creampuff and Cocoa? Was *she* the thief?

Nancy looked around for a place to hide

so she could keep tabs on Ella's phone call.

But it was too late. Ella turned around just then and spotted the three girls.

"I've gotta go," she said hastily. She snapped her cell phone shut. "Hey!" she called out to the girls, smiling nervously. "What's up?"

Bess marched up to Ella. "We heard you talking about Creampuff and Cocoa," she said. "'Fess up! Where are you hiding them?"

Ella's eyes widened. "Creampuff and Cocoa? I wasn't talking about Creampuff and Cocoa."

Nancy frowned. "But you were talking about two kittens from Furball Farm. Who else could it be?"

Ella giggled. "I, um, I was talking about these *other* kittens. See, um, I helped my friend Alice adopt two kittens from Furball Farm. But it turns out Alice's mom, um, doesn't like Terry for some weird reason. They used to, um, play tennis together or something. Maybe they had some sort of really bad fight about tennis—was the ball in, was the ball out, that sort of thing. I have no idea. I don't really like tennis. I like racquetball way better. Anyway, I was just telling Alice that she shouldn't tell her mom that these kittens came from Terry. Otherwise, her mom might send them back or something. . . ."

Ella was talking very fast. Nancy was having a hard time keeping up with what she was saying.

Ella's cell phone began to ring. She got a panicky expression on her face.

"Excuse me," Ella said. She clicked open the phone. "Hello?" she said. "Oh, hey, Mom! No, I'm at Furball Farm right now. What do you mean, I'm late? I thought that—"

Nancy motioned George and Bess closer. "Do you think Ella's telling the truth?" she whispered to her friends.

Bess shook her head. "She's acting super guilty."

"Like she's hiding something," George added.

Nancy nodded. "I agree. But why would she steal the kittens? If she knew someone who wanted to adopt them, she could have just asked Terry."

"True," Bess said.

Nancy grabbed Bess's and George's arms. "Come on. We need to talk to Terry. Right away."

"No, I didn't adopt out a pair of kittens recently," Terry told Nancy and her friends.

Terry was in her kitchen, loading up the dishwasher with cat food dishes. Nancy, Bess, and George had found her there and repeated Ella's story to her.

"And I don't play tennis," Terry went on. "And I don't know any friend of Ella's named Alice whose mother doesn't like me. Ella's story doesn't make any sense at all!"

Nancy pondered this for a moment. "Can you think of any reason why Ella would steal Creampuff and Cocoa?" she asked Terry.

Terry shook her head. "None at all. If she had wanted to adopt them, or if she knew of someone who wanted to adopt them, she would have just asked me. She wouldn't have taken them, like some sort of common thief! She's a good, responsible girl."

"Maybe we should talk to Ella again," George suggested to Nancy.

Nancy nodded. "That's a good idea. Ella might not be the thief. But she's sure hiding something."

Just then, Nancy saw Ella out the kitchen window. Ella was crossing the backyard and heading toward the street. She was walking very fast, almost running.

"There she goes!" Nancy said, pointing.

"Let's follow her," Bess said. "Maybe she'll lead us to the kittens."

"Definitely," Nancy agreed.

"I have to stay here and give Noodle and Fred their medication," Terry said. "Please call me as soon as you know anything!"

"We will," George promised.

The girls went out the front door, making sure that Ella wouldn't see them. Ella was walking down the street in the direction of downtown River Heights.

Nancy, George, and Bess followed her at a safe distance. Every once in a while they ducked behind a tree or a parked car so Ella wouldn't spot them. Ella was wearing a bright pink parka, which made her very easy to see against the snowy white landscape.

The girls followed Ella for five minutes,

then ten. She turned the corner onto Wesley Street and went into a tall brick building at 198 Wesley Street. The sign on the building said WESLEY NURSING HOME.

"A nursing home?" George said, surprised. "What's she doing at a nursing home?"

"Let's find out," Nancy said. She ran toward the front door, with George and Bess at her heels.

They entered a small lobby, painted in cheerful yellow and orange tones. A receptionist sat behind a desk. Her face was half-hidden behind a tall vase of red tulips. "Can I help you?" she called out to the girls.

"We're looking for a girl who just came in here. She was wearing a bright pink parka," Nancy said breathlessly.

"Oh, yes, Ella Gurney," the receptionist said. "She's here to visit her great-aunt Rosalie."

"She is?" Bess said.

The receptionist nodded. "Ella went that way. You can catch her if you hurry." She pointed down the hall.

Nancy thanked the woman and hurried

down the hall. The hall was empty, however. Nancy didn't see any sign of Ella.

Just then, she heard a familiar-sounding voice. "Here, kitties!" the voice rang out.

Nancy followed the sound. It was coming from Room 122. The door was open.

Nancy peeked into the room. The only person in the room was Ella. She was crouched down under the bed.

"Here, kitties!" Ella repeated. "Here, Creampuff and Cocoa!"

Nancy stepped into the room. "Ella Gurney, *you're* the cat thief!" she cried out.

8

The Kittens Are Found

Ella scrambled to her feet, bumping her head on the bed. "Ow!" she exclaimed. She rubbed her head. "What are you doing here?" she asked the girls, looking panicked.

"You're the cat thief we've been looking for," Nancy repeated angrily. "Where are they? Where are you hiding Creampuff and Cocoa?"

Ella's mouth dropped open. "I—I don't know what you're talking about," she sputtered.

"We heard you calling for them," Bess said, putting her hands on her hips. "Come on. Hand them over!"

Ella fell silent. Then she lowered her head. "Oh, all right," she said finally. "I'm your cat thief. But I'm not, really! I didn't steal the kittens. Not exactly, anyway. I just kind of, um, borrowed them."

"Borrowed them?" Nancy said, surprised.

Ella nodded. "Toward the end of Terry's open house. I thought I'd borrow them, and that nobody would notice if they were missing for an hour or two. I wanted to bring them here to show my great-aunt Rosalie. She used to have two cats that looked a lot like Creampuff and Cocoa. I figured it would cheer her up, because she's been kind of sad lately."

Nancy pondered all this. Ella seemed to be telling the truth. "But why didn't you just ask Terry if you could borrow them?" she asked Ella.

Ella shrugged. "I was afraid Terry would say no. I guess that was pretty dumb of me, huh?"

"Where are the kitties now?" Bess demanded.

"That's the problem," Ella confessed.

"They kind of, um, escaped from Great-Aunt Rosalie's room. I couldn't find them anywhere. I've been here every day, looking for them. I heard a rumor that they were living in the cafeteria and stealing leftovers. Then I heard a rumor that they were living with Mrs. Knowles in Room 342. I keep hearing all sorts of rumors. But I haven't been able to find them."

She added, "I thought I could just find them and sneak them back into Furball Farm. I didn't want to tell Terry that I lost them. I was afraid she would fire me."

Nancy glanced around. "I have a plan," she announced. "Ella, you're going to call Terry on your cell phone and tell her everything you just told us. At least she'll know that the kittens are here and safe. Bess, George, I need you to go to the cafeteria and get me some strawberries."

"Strawberries?" Bess and George said in unison.

Fifteen minutes later, Nancy, Bess, and George were walking down the second-floor hallway of the nursing home with several bowls of strawberries. Nancy had followed a trail of furballs, chewed-up magazines, and fresh, half-eaten granola bars to this wing of the nursing home. She figured Cocoa and Creampuff must be close.

"Cocoa!" Nancy called out. "Creampuff!" But there was no response.

A gray-haired woman poked her head out of one of the doors. "There's nobody by those names here," she rasped at the girls.

"We're looking for a couple of kittens," Bess explained.

The woman smiled. "Oh, those little rascals? They were just here. I think they went to visit Joyce Mains in Room 255."

"Thank you!" Nancy said.

The girls hurried down to Room 255. There was no one inside. There were no cats inside, either.

Nancy set down a bowl of strawberries in the doorway. She indicated to George and Bess that they should do the same, farther down the hall.

Then they waited. And waited.

After a while, Nancy heard a scurrying

noise coming from a side hallway. Seconds later a furry little figure appeared from around the corner. And then another. The two figures raced toward one of the bowls of strawberries and began sniffing eagerly. Then they started munching away.

Creampuff and Cocoa!

"We found them!" Bess hooted. "Kitties, we found you!"

Creampuff and Cocoa looked up briefly from their bowl of strawberries. Creampuff had a spot of red juice on her cream-colored nose. Then they went right back to their snack.

Nancy and the girls rushed up to the kittens and petted them happily. The kittens purred and continued eating.

That night Nancy curled up under the covers and pulled out her special blue detective notebook. She thought for a moment, tapping her purple pen against the notebook. Then she began to write:

Today we found Creampuff and Cocoa. They were living at the Wesley Nursing

Home. They snuck food from the cafeteria and hid from the authorities. But they also made a lot of friends there.

Terry was super glad that we found them. Ella apologized about a hundred times for what she did. Terry accepted her apology and even let her keep working at Furball Farm—as long as she promised to not sneak any more cats away for nursing-home visits without telling Terry first!

The senior citizens at the nursing home really loved having Creampuff and Cocoa living with them. Especially Ella's great-aunt Rosalie. In fact, Terry suggested that maybe the kitties could keep living there as house pets. The nursing home manager agreed.

So now Creampuff and Cocoa have a wonderful new place to live—together!

And Bess, George, and I have an awesome article for our school project about Terry, Furball Farm, and the mystery we solved!

Case closed!

COMING SOON:

Nancy Drew
and the ? Clue Crew

Nancy and her friends are
forming a detective club!

Join the Clue Crew on
their first case in
Summer 2006